P9-BYX-149

Rogers & Wilson

THE JELLYBEANS
and the Big Camp Kickoff

Jefferson Madison
Regional Library
Charlottesville, Virginia

BY LAURA NUMEROFF AND NATE EVANS

ILLUSTRATED BY LYNN MUNSINGER

Abrams Books for Young Readers, New York

30508 6884
R

The illustrations in this book were made
with watercolor on paper.

Library of Congress Cataloging-in-Publication Data

Numeroff, Laura Joffe.
The Jellybeans and the big camp kickoff / Laura Numeroff, Nate Evans;
illustrated by Lynn Munsinger.
p. cm.

Summary: When four friends with different talents and abilities go to summer
camp together, they use their strengths to make camp fun for all.

ISBN 978-0-8109-9765-3
[1. Camps—Fiction. 2. Friendship—Fiction. 3. Animals—Fiction.]
I. Evans, Nate. II. Munsinger, Lynn, ill. III. Title.
PZ7.N964Jf 2011
[E]—dc22
2010023698

Text copyright © 2011 Laura Numeroff and Nate Evans
Illustrations copyright © 2011 Lynn Munsinger

Book design by Chad W. Beckerman

Published in 2011 by Abrams Books for Young Readers, an imprint of ABRAMS. All rights reserved. No
portion of this book may be reproduced, stored in a retrieval system, or transmitted in any form or by
any means, mechanical, electronic, photocopying, recording, or otherwise, without written permission
from the publisher.

Printed and bound in China
10 9 8 7 6 5 4 3 2 1

Abrams Books for Young Readers are available at special discounts when purchased in quantity for
premiums and promotions as well as fundraising or educational use. Special editions can also be created
to specification. For details, contact specialmarkets@abramsbooks.com or the address below.

THE ART OF BOOKS SINCE 1949
115 West 18th Street
New York, NY 10011
www.abramsbooks.com

For Sophie, with love.
Welcome to our family!
—L.N.

For my wonderful stepdad, Jim,
who did a fine job raising a
wild and wacky pack of jellybeans!
—N.E.

Nicole loved to play soccer.

She practiced while cleaning her room.

She practiced while walking home from school.

And she even practiced while trying to fall asleep at night.

Nicole and her best friends, Emily, Anna, and Bitsy, were going to Camp Pook-A-Wow. Emily loved to dance, Anna loved to read, and Bitsy loved arts and crafts.

Before they left for camp, the girls stopped at their favorite place, Petunia's, and shared their favorite candy—jellybeans!

Just as jellybeans are different flavors but go well together, the girls were all different but got along great—and so they called themselves the Jellybeans, too.

The Jellybeans boarded the bus for camp.

"I can't wait to go on nature hikes," said Emily.

"I hope there aren't any bugs!" said Bitsy.

"I'm excited to sing campfire songs," said Anna.

"I want to play games!" Nicole said, balancing a soccer ball on her head.

When the girls finally arrived, they were greeted by Ms. Jangley-Cheezer, their camp counselor.

"Welcome to Camp Pook-A-Wow," Ms. Jangley-Cheezer said. "We're going to have a terrific summer. Now it's time to go swimming!"

The girls changed into their suits and joined the other campers by the lake. Nicole did a cannonball into the water. Emily dived gracefully. Anna swam the sidestroke. And Bitsy floated in an inner tube.

That night, they gathered around the campfire
and toasted marshmallows. "Yummy!" the Jellybeans
said. Then Anna read them ghost stories.

The next morning, Ms. Jangley-Cheezer told the Jellybeans about all the fun activities they could do at Camp Pook-A-Wow. "There is something for everyone," Ms. Jangley-Cheezer said.

Emily was thrilled that there was a dance class. She learned wonderful dances from other countries.

Bitsy went to the crafts room, where she made macaroni necklaces for her friends.

Anna read books about nature while
sitting under an oak tree.

But Nicole couldn't find anything that was just right for her.

"I want to play soccer," Nicole said.

"I'm sorry, Nicole. Camp Pook-A-Wow doesn't have a soccer team, but we have lots of other sports you could try," Ms. Jangley-Cheezer said.

KAYAKS

BADMINTON

TENNIS

SWIMMING

GYMNASTICS

ARCHERY

So Nicole tried tennis. She didn't like it.

Then she tried gymnastics.
She didn't like that, either.

Finally, Nicole tried kayaking.

But that was the worst of all.

"I miss playing soccer," Nicole said.

"I have an idea," Emily said. "Why don't we start our own soccer team?"

"That sounds great!" Bitsy added.

"I'll join the team, too," Anna said.

"What a wonderful idea," Ms. Jangley-Cheezer said. "Maybe we can play a game with Camp Mookie-Wanna."

"Let's start practicing!" Nicole shouted.

Nicole taught the girls how to dribble
and kick into the corner of the goal.

Anna read the rule book
and explained the game.

Emily played the goalie and leaped like a dancer.

Bitsy made uniforms.

The day of the big game arrived. The Jellybeans took their positions on the field.

The players on the Camp Mookie-Wanna team were big. *Really* big! Nicole started to feel nervous.

Ms. Jangley-Cheezer blew the whistle. "Let the Big Camp Kickoff begin!"

Nicole ran and kicked.

She passed the ball back and forth with Bitsy and Anna.

Emily made a daring save!

But the Mookie-Wanna team was just as good, and the score was tied. With one minute left in the game, Nicole charged down the field. She was in position for the winning goal. But she couldn't move.

"I don't think I can kick that far!" Nicole said.

"You can do it!" Emily shouted from the other end of the field.

"You're the best soccer player at Camp Pook-A-Wow!" Bitsy added.

"Go, Nicole!" Anna said.

Nicole heard her friends cheering and took a deep breath. She kicked the ball as hard as she could. It zoomed up, up, up!

"GOAL!" Ms. Jangley-Cheezer cried.
"Hooray for the Jellybeans and Camp
Pook-A-Wow!"

The girls hugged Nicole and jumped up and down.

"You were amazing," said Anna.

"Fantastic kick," added Bitsy.

After the game, Emily said, "I have a big surprise."
She pulled out a bag from Petunia's. "I've been saving
these for a special occasion."

"And this is it!" said Anna.

"Hooray for Nicole!" said Bitsy.

"Hooray for us!" shouted Nicole. "Hooray for . . ."

MAR   2011